I ♥ CHEESE

MACK
and the
Missing Cheese

THIS BOOK
BELONGS TO:

_ _ _ _ _ _ _ _ _ _ _ _ _ _ _

_ _ _ _ _ _ _ _ _ _ _ _ _ _ _

CHAE STRATHIE

NIKKI DYSON

MACK
and the
Missing Cheese

SCHOLASTIC

Once there was a **lovely piece of cheese** sitting on a plate, minding its own business.

Then it was **gone**.

No one knew where it went.

It was a mystery.

This was just the job for **Mack**.

Mack was the finest cat detective he knew.
His nose was always on duty and
his whiskers were finely tuned.

Or so he told his faithful assistant, **Squeak**.

Mack was the crime-fighting genius who had solved the cases of...

THE DISAPPEARING DOUGHNUTS

"STICKY 'EM UP!"

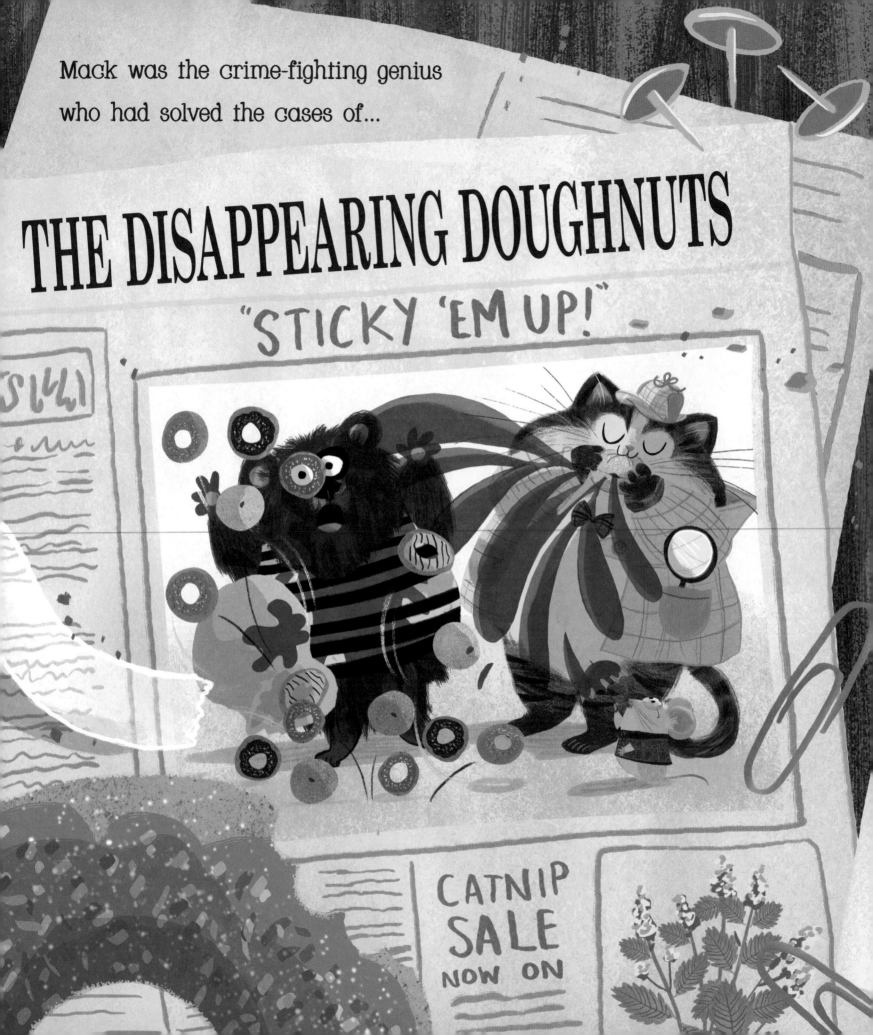

THE TERRIBLE TRICYCLE TYRANT

...and put the **Pesky Painting Pincher** in a pickle.

THE MONA CHEEZA

SQUEAK and the Thief.

If anyone could track down the **mysterious missing cheese**, it was Mack. Or so he told his assistant, Squeak. "Now, where's my magnifying glass?" said Mack.

"You're holding it," Squeak pointed out.
"So I am," chuckled Mack.

Mack examined
all around the plate.

"AHA!" he said.

"Oho!"
said Squeak.

Pawprints.

Mack already had several suspects in mind.

It was time to catch a cheese thief.

HUGE TROUBLE

BIG AND BAD

SNEAKY AND CHEEKY

SUSPICIOUSLY SMALL

And Mack knew exactly where to begin – with the meanest, most **terrifying** suspect of them all.

LITTLE BIRD, I believe YOU stole the cheese!

"I did not," cheeped Little Bird.

"HA! We have a trail of pawprints to prove it!" laughed Mack.

"Mack," whispered Squeak.

"What?" said Mack.

"She doesn't have paws," said Squeak.

Mack looked at Little Bird's feet.

"He's right," chirped Little Bird,
holding up a small foot.
"These are not paws."

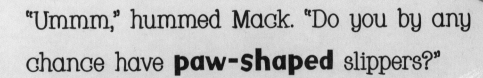

"Ummm," hummed Mack. "Do you by any
chance have **paw-shaped** slippers?"

"NO," chirped Little Bird.

"Oh," said Mack.
"Sorry to bother you," called Squeak.

Next on the list was Ginger Cat.

GINGER CAT, have you seen this cheese?

"Oh, I don't like cheese," purred Ginger Cat.
"I prefer my snacks a little more...furry."
She smiled a toothy smile at Squeak.

"I-I don't think it was her," gulped Squeak.

"We must question her further," said Mack.

Ginger Cat licked her lips.

"SHE DIDN'T DO IT!!"

Squeak yelped, and he dashed off as fast as his furry little legs would carry him.

There were three more suspects left on the list.

POODLE! Where were **you** when the cheese went missing?

"Fetching this stick," panted Poodle.

It was a good excuse.

SNIFF SNIFF

BOB

"This is not our man," said Mack.

"I can definitely smell **cheese**," said Squeak.

Rabbit was in the clear too...

SOLVED!

THE TERRIBLE TRICYCLE TYRANT

And Fox's new skateboard left **wheel**-prints, not pawprints.

Mack scratched his ear. "This is going nowhere, fast!" he grumbled.

CLACKALACKA!

"We could go back and follow the trail of pawprints," suggested Squeak.

"I know!" exclaimed Mack. "Let's follow the **pawprint trail!**"

"Great idea," muttered Squeak.

So they followed the trail.
Round and **round** they went,

past **Little Bird**...

Ginger Cat...

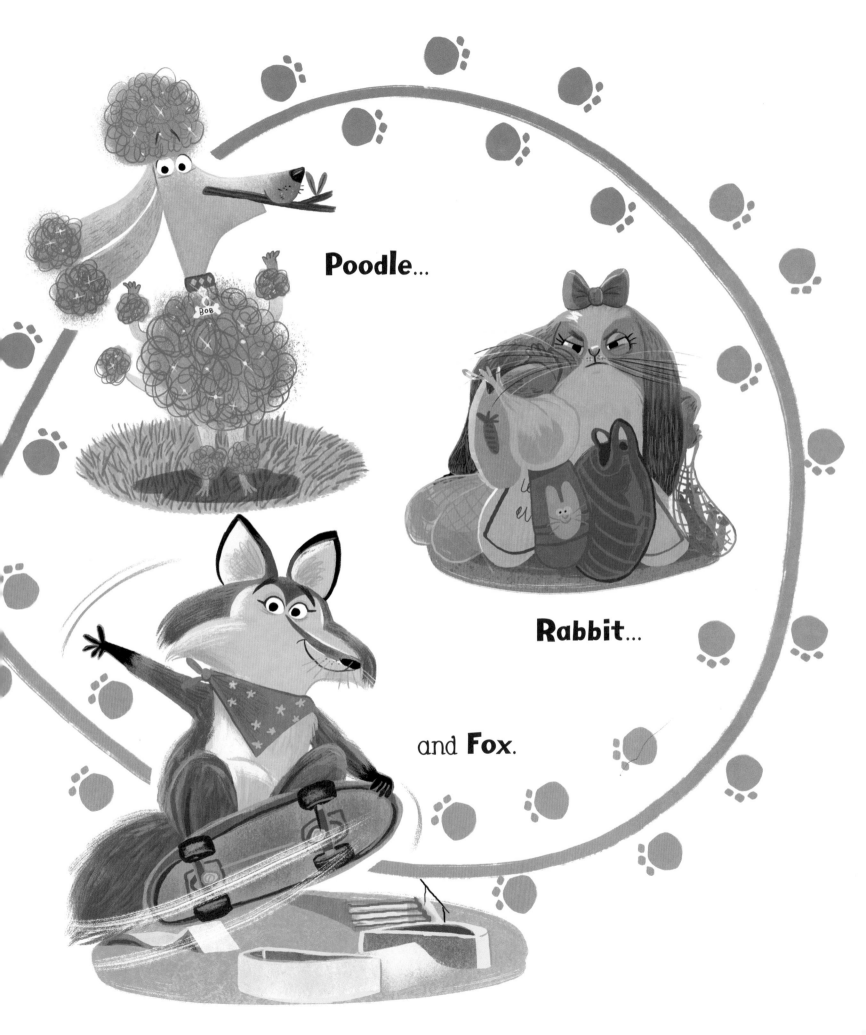

Poodle...

Rabbit...

and **Fox**.

"It feels like we're going in circles, Squeak," groaned Mack. "I don't think we'll **ever** solve this mystery – perhaps a **little nibble** will help us think."

CARE FOR SOME CHEESE?

BOING!

"Well **that** didn't help," said Mack. "I'm still stumped."

But Squeak didn't say anything.

MUNCH MUNCH

He was too busy peering at Mack's **pawprints**...

And that new **badge** on his jacket...

Hang on! Hadn't they just nibbled...

"Mack," said Squeak. "Where did you get that cheese we just ate?"

"From a plate," said Mack.

"The same plate that the **missing cheese** was on?" Squeak asked suspiciously.

"YES!" said Mack.

"How did you guess?"

"I think," sighed Squeak, "we may have solved the mystery."

"You could be right..." said Mack.

"...perhaps there never was a **cheese thief** after all..."

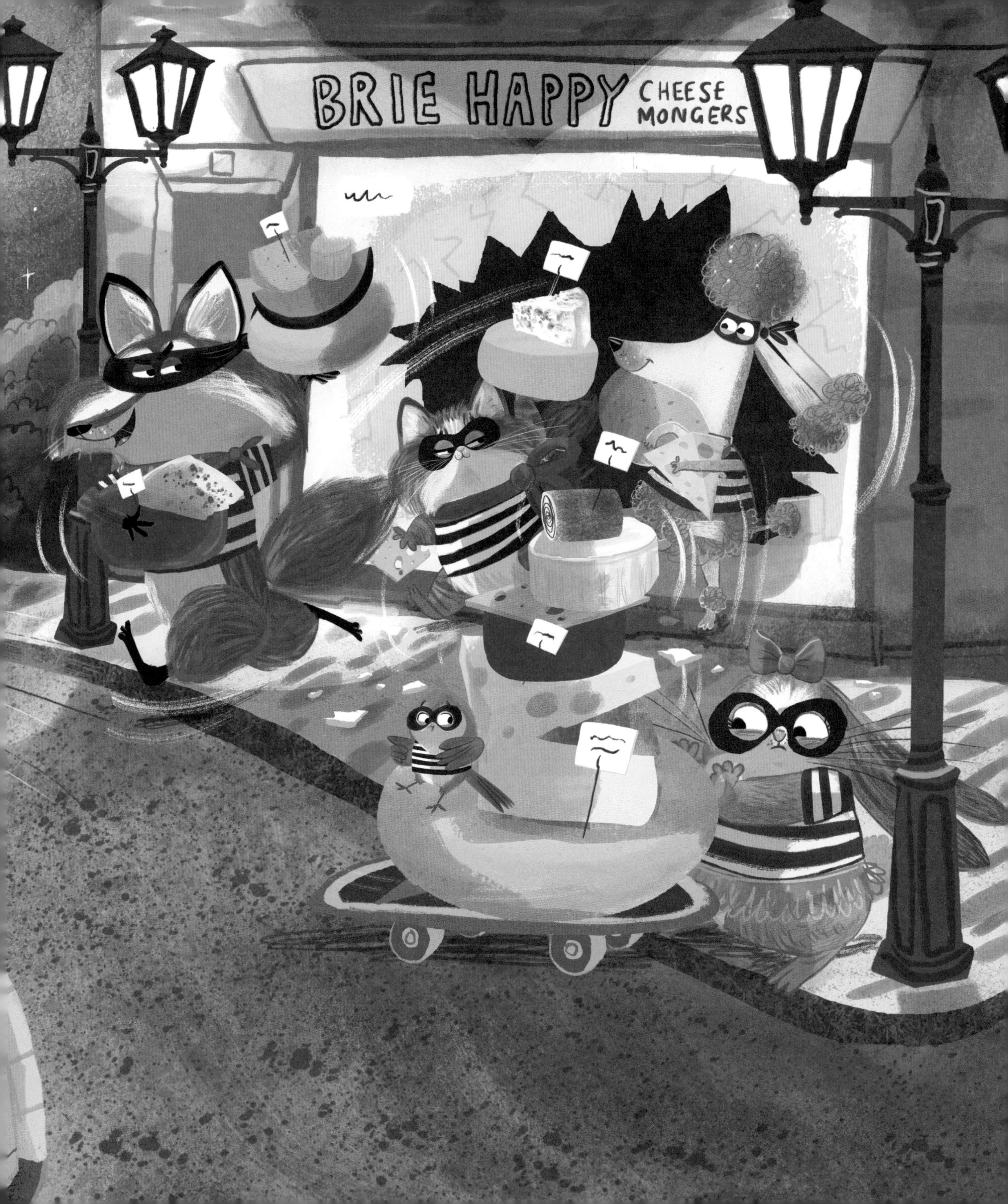
BRIE HAPPY
CHEESE MONGERS

For Elliot, the smallest
member of the family
(for now)
C.S.

For my brie-lliant Dad,
thanks for being so
grate! With love x
N.D.

First published in 2018 by Scholastic Children's Books
Euston House, 24 Eversholt Street
London NW1 1DB
a division of Scholastic Ltd
www.scholastic.co.uk
London ~ New York ~ Toronto ~ Sydney ~ Auckland
Mexico City ~ New Delhi ~ Hong Kong

Text copyright © 2018 Chae Strathie
Illustrations copyright © 2018 Nikki Dyson

PB ISBN 978 1407 16415 1

Papers used by Scholastic Children's Books are made
from wood grown in sustainable forests.